T0167281

THE CHRONICLES OF AN ORIGINAL

Dylan Wetzel

 www.trafford.com

North America & international
toll-free: 1 888 232 4444 (USA & Canada)
phone: 250 383 6864 ♦ fax: 812 355 4082

I'd like to thank my family for supporting me while I wrote my book, for always beliveing in me.

PROLOGUE

B *lood . . . so much blood,* I thought, trying to stop the bleeding. My hands are drenched in blood, pressed up against the gash on my stomach. The body of a black bear lay a few feet away, a spear lodged in its skull. The blood ran into my animal skin vest and trousers.

It had happened so quickly. I was hunting for deer and then, suddenly, the bear burst from the brush. Its paw smacked into my gut hard, claws tearing through my skin and flesh easily, slamming me into a tree. I barely had enough time to plunge my spear into its skull.

Yet, despite my strike, the bear had made a lethal blow. My blood was flowing out in torrents, vision blurring. I lay there, bleeding . . . dying. "Please," I whispered into the night, barely making a sound, "d-don't . . . let m-me . . . die. I'm not . . .

r-ready to die. Please. I'd . . . do a-anything . . . t-to live." Then, as if hearing my desperate, dying plea, a man appeared.

I instantly knew there was something . . . off . . . about him. He had short, dark black hair and his eyes . . . so black that it was like looking into a sea of never ending darkness. He has fair skin . . . completely covered in scares and burns. Some were long and deep looking, while others looked small and shallow. He wore an animal skin hide, reaching his knees, and as black as night.

Looking at him . . . I felt absolutely terrified. His scars screamed dangerous; his eyes, calm, calculative and full of menace. He grinned at my terror, revealing serrated perfectly white teeth.

Before I could speak, he tore my spear from the bears head easily, and tossed it beside me. Finally, he spoke in a hard, dangerously calm voice, "Do you really want to live? Are you willing to do anything?"

Still terrified, I somehow managed to whisper, "Yes."

He smiled, teeth glinting in the moonlight and said, "So be it." Faster than I could see or possibly imagine anyone able to move so fast, he sliced my neck and his palm open in one fluid motion. Then he placed his bleeding palm onto my neck, and I screamed out in pain.

His blood was like blazing white hot fire, instantly painful. I tried to hold back the pain, but it wasn't possible. Grinning like a pure madman, he held his palm against my open wound until my entire body was in pure agony. Faintly, I could smell blood, mine, his and the bears . . . and it was slowly making my throat burn. "There. Now, you'll live for all eternity. You'll craze fresh, living blood. You will need to drink or you'll become weak.

"You are a vampire, and so your greatest ally and true home will be in the darkness," he tells me. "And you are the first of the vampires. You owe me nothing, but remember my name, Lucifer."

x

CHAPTER 1

After countless millennia of blood and darkness, I thought, staring up at the moonless sky, *I still remember his name.*

"That's good to hear, my son," a familiar voice whispered somewhere behind me. Whirling up onto my feet, baring my fangs and hissing, all in less than a millisecond.

A low chuckle, and then he appeared. My father, creator. Lucifer. "Nice to see you as well, Dorian," he told me. I saw a dark, wry humor in his eyes. Something I never imagined to see from him. Unlike last time, he wore a dark, pitch black cloak and dress shoes, leather gloves.

"Where'd you come from?" I growled, relaxing somewhat. Though he was my father, the being who had given me new life, I knew he wasn't really a man. Of all the years I've walked this world, I'd heard countless tales about him. I knew they were all true just by being in his presence.

He grinned slightly, and says, "I am everywhere and nowhere, once the sun has set, my son." *It's not an all-out lie*, I thought. When I thought back to that night, it almost made sense. The sun had set long before he had arrived.

Casting him a questioning glance, I ask, "Why, after all this time, all these millennia, do you come to me tonight?" He smelled like smoke, ash, burnt flesh and death. In a way, he is all of those things.

His smile faltered for a heartbeat, and then his next words struck my heart hard. "I've come to give you a warning. You're one of six vampires who share my blood. You're the first, and so this problem falls to you.

"Over the millennia, you six spread vampirism all across the planet. But in this last century . . . two have been slain. Humanity is now purposefully seeking out Originals. They're hunting in large groups, up to twenty-five to thirty people. They use silver, garlic and ash wood stakes."

Anger and rage slowly burned threw me. I clenched my fists, trying to control myself. It didn't work, not at all. "I know what you're feeling. You're going to try and kill them all, and I have no intention of stopping you. But be careful," he tells me, slowly dissolving and fading away into the night.

A low growl escaped my lips, and I stalked off into the night, fury curling inside me, hell bent on killing every slayer that dared to stand in my way.

But . . . not while the thirst burns my throat life wildfire.

A small town was only a few moments away, across a few acres. The closer I got to the town, the stronger the smell got and my throat raged more and more. It was more intense than I'd felt it in a very long time. I hadn't fed in a few days, and I was truly ravenous.

But then the smell, so very, very tantalizing, become repulsing. But I knew that smell. That dangerous, lethal smell to vampires. It was raw garlic.

Immediately, I stopped breathing and exhaled, leaping up into a tree, near the top, and looking around, scanning the area with all my senses, trying to find the source of the smell. Within a few moments, I found it.

I hear multiple feet crunching on the ground, some much quieter than others. The slayers appeared, one by one, in a large group, wearing necklaces of pure, raw garlic. About twenty slayers all carrying different types of weapons. All capable of killing or seriously injuring a vampire.

Hardly daring to breathe, I inhale slowly, cautiously. The garlics scent is thick and heavy in the air, suffocating, but doesn't harm me.

CHAPTER 2

Breathing more deeply now, relaxing, I also smell . . . ash wood, silver and a lot of gunpowder. Closely examining the slayers, I notice the guns. Rifles, no less, presumably with silver, ash wood tipped bullets, and probably blessed with holy water.

But most of all, I smell their blood. Hot, delicious blood coursing through their veins. Then one of them, a far skinned man with short, light brown hair, medium set cheekbones and low set eyes, says, "Do you honestly believe we'll be able to kill another one of those . . . things?"

Silently as a ghost, I leap from branch to branch, getting closer to them. The thirst was blazing even greater now, their blood calling to me, my hunting instincts raging inside me, wanting to take over.

A redheaded man, most likely the leader of the bunch as they looked at him. He turned around and practically shouts, "Of course we are! We killed those Russian and German ones, didn't we? We're going to rid the world of these monsters once and for all!"

Maybe it was the threat of wiping out my species, or calling us monsters that made me leap behind him and snap his neck. In the blink of an eye, I leap back into the tree with his body, sinking my elongated fangs into his neck, puncturing an artery.

Rich, sweet blood gushed into my mouth and I eagerly gulped it down. As his body withered and dried, my own strength and Power grew.

The slayers, the moment I took their leader, went offensive. Guns were loaded and safeties clicked off, stakes at the ready.

Fools, I thought, tossing the body away. It gave a low thud as it hit the ground, and instantly a gun went off, the sound reverberating through the woods and I leapt forward swiftly, taking a young man to the ground.

Before he can react and alert the others, I slam my fist into his head, instantly knocking him out. I quickly sink my teeth into him and begin to feed again. As I drink, I hear angry shouts and people muttering . . . and quickly approaching footsteps.

"James, you goddamn idiot! Why'd you shoot?! These bullets aren't cheap or easy to come by, you know!!" a man yelled angrily, getting closer with each step.

Hissing silently, I drag the body into a nearby thicket, thick enough to conceal both me and the body. A moment later, the man who had spoken appeared. He's older than the others, around either his late forties or early fifties. Light gray hair framed his hardened face, with deep, dark eyes.

As I finished drinking, an idea came to me. Taking the clothes from the dead slayer, James, I slowly begin to reshape my own body. My short, black hair and dark emerald eyes with slight red dots turned long, reaching down to my shoulders, a light brown and dark sea blue eyes of James. My pale skin and light build pulsed and changed, making me look exactly like him. Nicely tanned skin and a muscular body.

Slowly getting to my feet, I crept away from the body and circled around the man. He smells like AB negative, absolutely delicious . . . if it wasn't for the scent of dead, truly and really dead, vampire blood. He was a veteran slayer, and had killed a great many vampires.

White-hot hatred surged through my entire body. I just barely managed to contain the snarl that was building deep in my chest. When I was sure I had enough control over myself, I step toward him. He glances at me, anger in his eyes. Takes a step forward, and then stops. "Where's your necklace, James?" he asks suspiciously, his deep voice wary.

Reaching inside the shirt, I pull out the peace of garlic which had been tied with a few strains of string, knowing he'd ask me. "Here, sir," I reply.

Still suspicious, or angry, perhaps both, he growled at me, "Fine. Okay. Back to the earlier issue of why you pulled the trigger and wasted a bullet on something that probably wasn't even a bird."

I didn't hesitate in my movement. Grabbing him by the throat, I lift him up off the ground and tried to toss him to the ground. He was surprised but didn't fall, like I had anticipated. He staggered a little, and then swung his fist towards me. I didn't even bothering trying to be defensive, or moving. His face slammed into my face, and his hand made aloud, satisfying crack as his bones cracked. He choked on a painful gasp and this time, I used a little more force.

Grabbing him by the throat again, I lifted him up a foot off the ground and slam him onto the ground. He grunts painfully and tries to shove me off. Annoyed, I break his arms and bash his head into the ground in one, violently swift movement.

Once I know he's unconscious, I feed yet again. But it's so, so much better. His blood is so, so sweet and delicious. Grateful, even, due to the fact that he was a slayer who had slain many of my brethren, and probably would've killed many, many more.

After a few minutes, his veins ran dry and his heartbeat had slowed too such an extent I could barely hear it. *Serves this right for fucking with a vampire,* I thought. My thirst now fully sedated, I began my long trek to a city where I know plenty of other vampires resided.

I didn't reach the town of Red Sapphire until dawn, even running at full speed. A mile or so back, I ditched the human clothes and disguise. A private club came into view, on the outskirts.

The owners were vampires. Ancients created by the other five Originals. I hadn't turned anyone yet because I haven't found the right person. They were also two of my closest friends in the immortal world.

The guard outside, a loyal human servant, knew who and what I was, so he didn't argue when I stepped by him and went inside. It was a sanctuary for vampires.

A bar that completely served our palate. Willing donors were always on hand; bottled blood, sometimes spiked with wine, and spiced with cinnamon or other herbs. It also had rooms for those of us who were tired of always being on the move.

Sitting in the very back were the owners. Ancients who had been turned in the year twenty-two thousand BCE. Sensing my presence, they looked around, trying to find me. The moment they did, I nodded as I quickly moved towards them.

"Welcome, Dorian," said the one on the right. His name's Ethan. Tall, long blond with blue highlights hair and ice blue eyes. He wore a long, richly dark black cloak and dress shoes.

"It's been a long time," the other said. Named Nathan, he had cropped pitch black hair, deep set dark hazel eyes with long lashes. Unlike Ethan, he wore a dark black t-shirt, trip-pants with chains and red straps, and combat boots.

Nodding apologetically, I say, "I've been meaning to stop by. Maybe I'll get a permanent residence here."

They smile lightly and gesture for me to take a seat. A moment after I do a vampiress offers me a drink. Declining, I shake my head, still full from my earlier feast.

Once she leaves, Ethan asks, "So tell us, what brings you here? You're a man, a vampire, who always seems to have something going on."

For a few moments, I'm silent. Then I tell them, "Slayers have been growing in larger and larger numbers. They seek us, and plan to wipe us out, one by one. On my way here, I ran into a group."

They're eyes widened in surprise. "You killed them, yes?" asked Nathan nervously.

"Of course I did. The main leaders, at least. The others shouldn't bother us again. But only a single group. They're all over the world, seeking us out.

They hunt with silver, ash wood stakes and tipped silver bullets, along with garlic," I tell them.

They look away, a slight hint of fear in their eyes. An emotion we almost never felt. Slayers were a worry in small groups, yes. But gathering in larger numbers? That was truly fearful. Especially when the truly experienced slayers gathered. They were a problem.

In order to reassure them, I say, "I'm not going to simply sit by and let them hunt us down anymore." They looked up, startled at the barely hidden anger in my voice. "It's time to protect my race. I'll show them that we won't simply let them kill us off one by one." My fists were clenched, thirst blazing again.

Ethan and Nathan were silent for a few moments before replying, "We're coming to help you."

CHAPTER 3

I was silent for a moment, wondering if they had fully thought this through. "Dorian, we know that'll be dangerous. But they're our people, too. It's just as much our duty to protect them as it is yours. Besides, you'll need help with this. We are willing to help you," Nathan told me.

He's right, I thought. The Ancients and the Elders just like the other Originals, ruled vampire kind. We were the authority and had to remain alive, but also to remain a myth to humanity.

They both remained silent as I thought it over. Finally, a few moments later, I agree. "You're right. We'll start the hunt once the sun sets." They nodded, fully confident about helping me.

"We should feed before leave, no? To be sure we're ready for the challenges that lie ahead," Ethan said.

"I agree," Nathan said. Both their eyes were darkening with thirst. We would gorge ourselves on the rarest, richest human blood.

"Then let's drink. We'll all need to beat our best. Will we drink and drain donors, or drink from the bottled blood you have?" I ask them, my eyes slowing beginning to blaze blood red.

"Fresh blood is the best, especially from the source. It's also more strengthening to kill, so we shall," Ethan said, walking down a dark hallway, me and Nathan following him.

Reaching the end, he opened a door, and we descended down a spiral stairway. The further we went down, the darker and colder it became. But it wasn't noticeable to us.

A few minutes later, we came to another door. Silently, we entered, one after the other. Inside, the walls were a dark, blood red. Low quality lights hung on the ceiling. Large, comfortable looking beds were scattered about, with red sheets, covers, and pillows.

Moments later, three humans appeared, and the middle one, a young man in his twenties with short, light blue hair and deep set bright green eyes, said, "Ah, masters Ethan and Nathan." Glancing at me, he quickly added, "And lord Dorian! Welcome." He gave us a low bow, as did the other two.

"Alex, me and Nathan shall be leaving at nightfall with Dorian. Until we return, William will be in charge," Nathan informed him, and he nodded. "Now, before we rest, we need to feed. Gather the donors who're willing to die in feeding for us."

"Yes, milord," Alex replied, walking away into a nearby room. A moment later, twelve humans walked out, Alex and the two other servants not among them.

They all smelled so very good. Almost all of them were either AB positive or positive. The smell was almost overpowering, thirst raging like a white hot wildfire and growing stronger.

Randomly selecting four each, we took a bed to feed on. The moment we sat, I sank my fangs into a women's neck, gulping down mouthfuls of blood. Within a few moments, she ran dry. Tossing the withered-up corpse away, I continued feeding.

By the time I'd finished draining the third human, I was practically stuffed. The fourth was quite beautiful, for a human woman. Tall, 5'3", and skinny, pale, with long, lustrous blonde hair frames her beautiful face with ice blue eyes.

"Tell me, human, what's your name?" I ask her. Looking around, I note that Ethan and Nathan have drunken their fill, are now deep asleep.

She looks at me, her expression tired and scared. "R-Raven, milord," she replied quietly.

"A lovely name . . . for a lovely human," I tell her, and reach forward to stroke her cheek. The instant my skin touches hers, a wave of electricity shoots threw us both. She cried out in surprise and I leap back a few feet. My fingertips still tingle from the brief contact.

"What . . . the hell was that?" I muttered to myself.

A soul bond, Dorian, Lucifer's voice said within my mind.

Pray tell, what exactly is this soul bond you speak of? I ask him. I should've been surprised that I could talk to him in my head with my thoughts, but it didn't. Not in the least.

He answers, *The bond between mated souls. Soul mates, Dorian. It seems you finally found yours.*

I snarled mentally. *You actually me expect me to believe this?!*

The proof is there when you touch her, son. She is your soul mate. All you have to do to prove it to yourself is too taste her blood, he tells me. Then I feel his presence within my mind vanish.

Shaking my head, thoughts in scrambles, I approach and sit down next to her. With the little space between us, I could feel the electricity. It flows over my skin gently. Looking into Raven's eyes, I noted that she could feel it as well.

"Raven, do you want to die? Or do you want to turn and live by my side forever?" I ask her quietly.

Half a heartbeat later, she replies, "I . . . want to live," and looks into my eyes. Her so very beautiful eyes, hair like snow. Tilting her head in a way that exposes her neck, the blood pulsing in her artery strongly. I lean forward and gently bite into her neck, blood rushing into my mouth. The electrical feeling flooded over us both, but we knew what to expect.

Within moments, she was on the verge of death. "This is going to hurt . . . a lot," I tell her, cutting open my palm with a fang, willing it to stay open and bleeding. I focused completely on keeping the wound open.

When the blood was flowing freely, I placed my bleeding palm onto her punctured neck. She cringed in pain, going rigid in my arms. But she didn't scream. Pulling her close, knowing it was going to be a long night, I close my eyes . . .

I'm the first to wake that evening. Looking at Raven, I'm pleased to see that she's fully gone through the change. But she doesn't smell like a normal vampire, or like an Ancient. But the answer was completely obvious.

I had given her enough of my blood to pass down everything I'd seen and done. *She's an Original now,* I thought. Comparing her scent to mine and Ethan's, it was more like mine.

Gently rising to my feet, I lay her onto the bed and head upstairs. I wasn't thirsty, wouldn't need to feed again in a couple of days. But I knew she would need to drink.

Alex sat behind the bar, reading a book. Noticing my approach, he put the book down, a rueful smile on his face and asked, "What can I do for you, master Dorian?"

"Four bottles of fresh blood clean," I replied. Those new to the thirst needed fresh, pure blood. He nodded, and went into a backroom. A moment or so later, he reappeared with the blood.

"Is there anything else you need, or is this it for now?" he asks.

"This should be enough for now. Thank you, Alex," I tell him, taking the bottled blood. He smiles sincerely, and I head back downstairs. Somehow, I know she's awake. Moments later, I reenter the room.

Raven looks up, and is instantly standing before me. "Blood?" she asked me. I nod lightly, and give her a bottle. She quickly opens it and drains it within seconds. About a minute and a half later, she's drained them all. Her eyes have shifted colors. They went from being a dark, dark blue, almost ocean black, to being a few shades darker than her normal eye color. "I'm still thirsty," she said, leaning against me. That same electrical feeling was back, but we were used to it. Even accepted it.

Wrapping an arm around her, I whisper, "I know. The thirst is always strongest the first few years. Eventually, it becomes easier to handle, and sedate."

We lay on the bed for what felt like hours, wrapped in each other's arms. But in reality, it was only a few moments. Her cool skin was like satin against mine, soft and slightly warm.

Minutes passed, and then Ethan and Nathan awoke. Instantly, they looked from to Raven in surprise.

CHAPTER 4

"You . . . you finally turned a human?" Ethan asked me, eyeing Raven from head to toe. She either didn't seem to notice, or was ignoring him.

"Yeah," I replied, narrowing my eyes at Ethan. Noticing, he stopped eyeing her and focused on me. "All the others have turned humans. It only took me a few millennia to find the right one," I added.

Ethan and Nathan exchanged glances, deep in thought. Then Nathan asks, "Why her, though? What does she offer our species that no other human could? What makes her so special?"

"I'm his mate," she growled, wrapping an arm around. "He's mine."

"And she's mine," I said. Then I pulled her close, and laid my head on top of hers. Her hair is like the finest silk. "Are you two ready to go yet or do you want to keep questioning me about why I turned her?"

That made them refocus on the objective ahead. "Give us a few minutes," Nathan said as we entered the main part of the building. I nod, and then he and Ethan briefly depart. They rejoined us a few moments later, carrying large black bags and a few set of daggers.

"What's in the bags?" Raven inquires as the four of us head out into the night. The horizon was slightly bright, indicating that the sun had just set.

"Bottles of blood wine, medical tools, armor if we need it," Ethan replies. Raven nods her head, understanding. Within minutes, after we passed the last traces of humanity, we all sit down, discussing what to do now.

"So Dorian, what should we do from here? What's our next step in hunting them down?" Ethan asks me. I sit across from him, listening to the sounds of the night. Nathan and Raven had gone out to hunt a few minutes earlier.

After a few moments of silence, I say, "I know someone up in Alaska who has connections all over the world. Both human and vampire. She should be able to help us."

He thought it over for a moments, and as he was, the others returned, their lips stained red with blood. As they sit down, Ethan asks, "Are you sure we can trust this friend of yours? If she is friends with humans as well, she could be providing the slayers with Intel on us."

I smirk slightly ad reply, "She's another Original. I've known her for a very longtime. I trust her as much as I trust you all right here."

Ethan blinked in surprise, and then nodded, trusting me. Having not heard the rest of the conversation, Raven inquires, "Whose place are we going to? What's been decided?"

"Dorian has suggested that we go to Alaska first. He has a friend up there, apparently an Original, who has connections among both humans and vampire kind. So how vote you?" Ethan said.

Together, almost at the exact same time, both Nathan and Raven said, "Aye."

Getting to his feet, he says, "Well, what are we waiting for? It's a long run to Alaska from here. We should get going now, while the going is good."

In an instant, everything changed. I tugged Ethan down to the ground, hidden in the darkest shadows. A group of hunters had appeared, and they seemed to suspect we were still around. *Shit*, I thought. *I barely had enough time to get Ethan hidden before I noticed they were coming. How could I be so careless? We need to focus, now more than ever.*

The slayers looked around desperately, trying to locate us. One shouted, "Where are they?! Does anyone know where they are?!"

A man slapped him and calmly said, "Incompetent fool. For all we know, they're long gone."

CHAPTER 5

"Well it seems they brought the hunt to us, eh, Dorian?" Nathan chuckled, licking his lips as their scent was carried to us by the gentle breeze. Altogether, it ranged from A positive to O negative.

A glance at Raven told me the smell was making her thirsty again. Animal blood never seemed to work for us. It wasn't as good, or as filling, as human blood is. She wasn't the only one either. Glancing at Ethan and Nathan, I could tell the thirst was growing.

Honestly, I was getting thirsty myself. My throat slowly began to burn and ach, my gums pulsing, fangs ready to come out. Swallowing didn't help, or make the pain go away. It actually seemed to do the opposite.

"Well?" I muttered, the thirst now blazing white-hot. "Are we going to kill them, or let them keep hunting and killing us off?"

"No way in hell," said Ethan, seeming to regain himself for a moment. "If we don't' kill them now, they'll only kill more and more of us. They have to die. It's our duty to kill them, at any coast and by any means necessary."

Nathan and Raven nodded their heads in agreement, and within half a heartbeat, we're circling them, analyzing our prey, searching for weaknesses among the slayers. Ten slayers all armed with the usual slayer tools and garlic of course. To me and Raven, it wasn't that bad.

"What do we do now?" one of them asked. No one got the chance to respond.

We all leapt forward, in unison, an eighth of a second later. The slayers had no time to react. All of us took two humans, drinking from them till the point of death and ripping their throats open.

Only two remained, frozen with absolute terror. "What should we do with them?" Raven asked, her eyes a misty blue.

"We could simply kill them. They deserve nothing more," Nathan suggested, licking his teeth and gums clean. "I mean, after all, who knows how many of us they've killed?"

That sparked a bit of fury deep within me. Looking at Raven, I ask her, "Are you still thirsty?" She quickly nods her head, eyes quickly turning dark red. "Kill them." The words seem to unfreeze them, and they try to run.

Almost instantly, however, I and Ethan force them to your knees, necks exposed. Raven quickly leans down and bites down into a man's neck. Seconds later, she moves to the second, a young woman. The woman whimpers as she gets closer, and goes still the moment Raven bites her.

Once she was finished, she stood up, blood dripping from her lips and asked, "So, are we going or what?" I looked around the clearing, the dead, bloodless bodies lying around.

"Ethan, Nathan, maybe we should do something about all these bodies?" I suggest. "So if anyone, by chance comes here, they won't find a bunch of dead, bloodless corpses."

It didn't take much time for them to think it over before nodding their heads in agreement. Quickly and effortlessly, we did a large hole in the ground, seven feet deep and nine feet wide. Then we toss the bodies in, and began to refill the hole with dirt, covering the bodies.

"There," sighed Ethan, once the ground was flattened. "Now can we get moving?"

"Yeah, we can. But we'll need a plane," I reply. "You two wouldn't happen to have a private jet or something, would you?"

They exchanged glances, before Nathan says, "We do. It's ready to leave whenever we are. It's only about a mile or so from here."

Nodding, I ask, "Are the windows tinted?"

"They're as darkly tinted as possible," Ethan tells me. "Follow us. We know where it is from here. Piloted by more of our loyal human servants."

"Well by all means, lead the way," I said, gesturing.

He and Nathan gestured, moving forward. Raven and I follow, hand in hand, into the darkness.

We walked in silence for a while, the night silent except for the scurrying of animals and the other nocturnal animals.

Moments later, we enter another clearing. This one, however, has buildings, and a sleek, jet black private jet.

CHAPTER 6

A small set of stairs led up the airshaft. Feet away from it was a small building, the hanger. There was also a cabin like building next to it. It could house at least ten to fifteen people easily.

The main cabin door opened, and three humans came out, approaching us. "This is private property. Leave now . . ." one started to say, a scowl on his face, but as they got closer, it turned into a smile. "Ah, masters Ethan and Nathan. It's been awhile. Welcome." The three bowed, respectfully.

"Marius, John, Erik," Nathan greets them, nodding at each as he does. Then he gestures to me and Raven. "This is the Original, Dorian, and his newborn mate, Raven." Smiling politely and formally, they give us a bow as well. "Is the jet ready? We need to be going soon."

The middle man, John, replies, "Yes, milord. The tank is full, engine and everything else at full. Where do you wish to go?"

Glances at me for half a moment, then back at John and says, "Alaska."

"Wait here," Erik says, and the three disappear back into the cabin. Moments later, Marius and another human appear. The other one tells us, "I'm Alexander and I'll be one of your pilots today. Now, let's get going."

We all climb up into the plane and within ten minutes, we're in the air.

We arrive in Alaska a few minutes before sunrise, so we just decide to sleep on the plane. The last thing I remember before falling asleep with Raven in my arms is a cold chill burning within my blood . . .

It's what woke me at dusk. The chill had grown so much worse. My veins felt like they were frozen solid, colder than ice.

Easily and gently, I get up without awakening Raven, and look out the window. The horizon is slowly growing darker.

But that isn't what caught my attention. It's the woman, standing only a couple of feet away, and gazing at the window I'm looking threw.

She was looking at me.

Short, light brown hair and beautiful light brown eyes, gleaming red dots and very pale skin. To pale for a human.

Silently, I open the door and jump down to the ground, then stood and faced her. I could instantly tell she was a vampire. But she was the Original I'd come here to see. Grinning, I said, "Nice to see you again, Jordan."

She smiles back and says in her sweet, rich voice, "Likewise, Dorian." She walks forward and asks, "How long has it been since we last met?"

I thought about it for a moment and reply, "Probably around two or three centuries." Thinking back, I realize that the burning chill was a signal that another Original was nearby. Sighing, I add, "But I come to you now with a motivation, a mission, and your connections will help me."

"What're you up to? You have . . ." she inhaled deeply, and continued, "two Ancients with you and a newborn Original." She gives me a very questioning glance.

"It'd be easier to tell you later, when the others are awake as well," I say. "Besides, he probably already told you and the others."

She shudders at the mentioning of our creator. "You're hunting the slayers, and need me to us my connections to find all the large groups, don't you?" she asked.

I nod my head. "I've already had a few encounters with them. They need to be stopped. If I don't stop them, they'll hunt us all down to the brink of extinction. If you help me, I will protect our kind. Not one slayer shall be spared," I say quietly.

She chuckles lightly. "I know you will, Dorian. You have a point as well. If we are to survive, then the slayers, all of them, must be killed.

"I'll do what I can to help you all in this quest," she declares. "Wake the others, and come with me."

I did as she said. First Raven, then Ethan and Nathan. "Why'd you wake us?" Ethan yawned.

"Because it's time to go. She's here," I tell him, leading them out. "Ethan, Nathan, Raven, this is the Original, Jordan. Jordan, these are the Ancients Ethan and Nathan. My mate, Raven."

She nods at them and smiles as they do the same. "So, shall we get going, then?" I ask her."

"Yes. Follow me, and we can discuss these matters somewhere private," she says.

CHAPTER 7

We walked in complete, utter silence. The night's deadly quiet, as if the entire forest was a graveyard. No animals were scurrying about, no birds or flying about. Even the wind was silent.

Minutes dragged by slowly, but after about ten minutes or so, we came to her mansion. It is huge. At least a hundred and twenty feet by a hundred and fifty feet.

"Well damn," whispered Ethan, gazing at the mansion. "Is all of this . . . yours?" he asks in awe.

"Yes," she replies with a slight smile. "It's a third blood bank, a third private club, and the last third is my personal sleeping chambers and management office. She nodded at us and continued heading towards the mansion. Already, we could hear the beating of heavy music and hearts thudding, and the sweet, sweet smell of adrenaline filled blood. It's rich and delicious, warm and inviting. With each step we take, the scent grows stronger. Not just human blood either. Vampire blood was mixed within it.

The moment Jordan opens the door; it's like a thunderous tsunami crashing down upon us. The smell of humans and vampires was powerful. Almost intoxicating.

Quickly, Jordan leads us to a chamber, and the smell and sound lessened instantly and immensely. We all sighed in relief. Looking around, I noticed we were in what appeared to be a meeting room.

A long silver table surrounded by chairs. *More like a discussion room,* I thought, taking a seat. Silently, the others took a seat, and Ethan and Nathan passed out large, spherical goblets and then filled them to the brim with blood wine.

Taking a large gulp, I was pleased to discover its AB negative, mixed with a small amount of cinnamon. "So, down to why we're here," I remind her.

She nods and says, "Yes of course. Dorian has told me why you're here. I know that the slayers are growing in numbers.

"You're here because of my connections around the world. You don't where to look or start. Dorian intends to wipe out all the slayers worldwide." She glances at all of us before adding, "I will help you in your quest."

All of us smile and say in unison, "Thank you. She smiles back and excuses herself to make a phone call. As I lift the goblet to drink, Raven speaks.

"Will we be hunting all across the world? Taste different blood?" she asks me, refilling her goblet again. Probably for the third or fourth time.

"Yes, love," I replied, kissing the top of her head after setting my goblet down onto the table.

Nathan says, "Where do you suggest we should start hunting at?" There's an eager gleam in eyes. The desire to hunt and kill.

"I'm not sure yet," I answer. "We've already began to hunt them here in the States. It'd be best to kill all of them here, and then we can move onto Europe." They think it over for a few moments then nod.

A moment later, Jordan reenters the room.

"There aren't that many around here. Maybe two or three groups left. There were more. Five at the most, but I'm just assuming you took care of them," she says, taking a seat. "Then you can go to Africa, and make your way up to Europe, and east to China." We all nod in acknowledgment.

"So how many groups are left outside America? How many must we kill?" Raven asks, finishing yet another goblet. I drink while Jordan thinks, draining it in seconds.

As I refill my goblet, Jordan replies, "Probably around six. Around nine at the most. They range from ten to twenty slayers per group."

Raven and I almost choke on the blood. "Ten to twenty per group?!" Ethan gasped. "That's insane!"

"I agree, but alas, it's true," Jordan sighs.

I sigh and say, "It doesn't matter how many there are. They'll die soon enough."

"When do we start the hunt again?" Nathan asked, drinking lightly from his half full goblet.

"In two days' time," I reply after a moment of thought. "To feed and to rest, and then we'll continue." I finished the blood, take Raven's hand and ask Jordan, "Do you have any spare rooms we can use? Where the sounds and smells of the club won't reach?"

She nods politely. "Guest housing is in the basement. Cool, but comfortable. There's only enough light for us to see by. No human can see down there, and it's never touched by sunlight," she answers, gesturing to a door behind her.

"Thank you," I tell her as Raven and I go through it. Too our immediate right is a stairwell. As we descend, the light and temperature, too us as vampires, just barely drops. Minutes pass, and then we reach a corridor.

It's long, as least ten to twelve feet wide and five feet wide. On both sides are silver doors.

Opening the first door on the right, it revealed a bright, white room. A large queen sized bed with huge, white pillows. A large TV, like we'd use it.

Sighing lightly, I lay on the bed, Raven beside me. Within seconds, she was sound asleep in my arms. A moment after she fell asleep, I, too fall asleep.

The two days passed like a breeze. We spent a little while with Jordan before we finally left to continue our quest.

CHAPTER 8

O nly about three hours had passed since we left Jordan's. Hundreds of miles away by now, probably. We had come meters into a slayer camp. We were close. Very close.

"Spread out and wait for the command," I whisper to them once the bonfire is within sight. The smell of dead vampire blood lingers from the camp.

The four of us linger far enough from the camp so we aren't seen, but close enough so we can what's happening. A few slayers stand around the edges of the camp, keeping watch. "Take the guards first, quietly, and then move deeper into the camp. See anyone that isn't one of us, kill them. Search the tents as well. We kill them all, no mercy," I whisper, knowing they could hear.

Slowly creeping forward, I note that three guards in sight. *Perfect,* I thought. *A guard for each of us.* Closing the distance to about five or six feet, I leap and take him to the ground, covering his mouth. Slowly I bite into his neck, smelling his terror and making his blood that much sweeter. A positive, I was sure, drinking deeply.

Within seconds, his body dries up, heart unable to pump blood. I pull away from the corpse, stronger and more powerful. Slowly and quietly, I approach a nearby tent. As I'm about to open it, a light click comes from within. I whirl to the side, hiding myself in shadows. The muzzle of a gun comes out, ready to fire, then a man. He's in his forties, white hair and gray beard. He'd garbed himself in a brown duster, flannel shirt and sweat pants.

"Where the bloody hell did Gregory go? That foolish amateur shouldn't go wondering into the night," the man muttered darkly.

"Ah, forget him John. If he's dead, we can simply recruit more," a voice said from within the tent. "Besides, there are plenty of others, more experienced slayers, who can help."

More experienced? I thought. *It'd be best to keep him alive and question him later*, I added to that thought. Moving as quickly as I can, I snap the man named John's neck, rushed into the tent and slam my fist into the others man skull.

Quickly, I drain John and drink from the other, but not to the verge of death. Just enough to keep him weak.

Leaving him there, I silently move from tent to tent, draining and breaking necks along the way. It isn't until I stumble upon the others that I realize that we'd finished here. Raven's licking the remaining blood from her lips and teeth when I tell them "Follow me."

They do without questioning me. I lead them to the human, dragging him out of the tent by his hair. He'd regained enough consciousness to cringe slightly.

"Why'd you leave one of them alive? You were the one who told us to kill them all," Ethan said.

"Unless they have valuable information we can use," I counter. "This pathetic, disgraceful creature knows more experienced slayers. He may even know where they are."

The three of them look at me, then him. Nathan growls light, Ethan's eyes narrow and Raven simply leans against me. Sighing impatiently, Nathan growled, "When the hell is he going to wake up?!" He grabbed the man's collar, lifted him up and slapped him across the face.

We all heard a few bones break, but it does what Nathan wanted. The human woke up.

The moment he sees us he screams, "Vampires!!" and reached for his stake. Ethan and Nathan grabbed and twisted both his arms. He cringed in pain, looking around for help.

"No one is here to help you. They're all dead," I tell him. At first, he seems stunned. Then he glares at all of us. Grinning, I continue. "You'll die as well, soon enough. But how you die is entirely up to you."

"I'm not going to tell you monsters anything!" he shouted angrily, struggling to break free.

"Se we'll do this the hard way then? So be it," I sigh slightly and nod at Ethan and Nathan. They grin and twist his wrists until they crack loudly. The man gasps put in pain loudly, holding back the scream as best as he could. Tears well up in his eyes. But he keeps glaring at us. Then a louder crack as they break his elbows. Tears run down his cheeks and he groans painfully.

I gesture at them to stop temporarily, and ask, "Had enough yet? Will you talk now, human? Or do you need to suffer more?"

Panting, he replies painfully, "N-no . . . matter w-what . . . you do . . . I w-will not . . . tell you . . . a-anything." He has a defiant look on his face, but we all could smell his fear. I took advantage of that fear. Looking directly into his, unblinking, I channel Power threw my eyes and voice as I say, "Tell me where these more experienced slayers are at, or we will tear you apart slowly."

His eyes go wide, slightly glazed as he answers, "Most should be in Philadelphia, at least five or ten. The other two . . . should be in Europe." When he finishes speaking, I snap his neck.

"What do you think we should do? Philadelphia, Europe, or the remaining slayer groups here?" I ask them.

"The experienced slayers and then the last few groups here and finally move out," Raven suggests.

Ethan smiles and says, "That's actually a pretty good plan." Glancing at Nathan, he nods his head.

"Then we shall go with that," I agree.

CHAPTER 9

We reach Philadelphia a few nights later. It's a pretty big city, at least.

It was sunset, and people were wondering about. To us, the thick, sweet aroma is very appealing. We all knew the easiest way to find the slayers: take a human into a dark alley and try to feed. We all agreed to give it a try.

We all split into two groups. Raven and I northern part, while Ethan and Nathan hunted in the southern part.

We found ourselves a decently middle-aged business man and took him into the nearest alley. It was dark, cold and most importantly, deserted. The perfect place to feed.

Dylan Wetzel

We both bit into his neck, slowly drinking away his life. He ran dry within a minute, but it was enough time. Four figures stood side by side in the alleyway entrance. Each held a silver stake, and their faces were cold, hard, displaying no emotions at all.

I smirk. "Let's have some fun with this," I tell Raven, and we leap forward. A stake whips forward, just barley brushing against my cheek.

My fist connects with his lower jaw, and he staggers back a few feet and another takes his place. His stake flies forward, aimed at my heart. I grab him by the wrist and break it. He doesn't flinch as he swings the other stake. I quickly dodge it and snap his upper arm. Pulling him close, I begin to feed.

The other slayer charges, stake posed for my right shoulder.

Tearing open his throat, I shove the body at the charging slayer. He moves to avoid colliding with it and I leap at him. Grabbing him by the throat, I lift him up off the ground and then slam him, head-first, onto the ground. Once his eyes roll into the back of his head, I quickly begin feeding.

Distinctively, I was aware of a scuffle behind me. But I didn't need to look. Raven had joined the fight.

When I finished, I glance at her and grin. Both of the slayers she had dealt with lay at her feet, bled dry. Her lips glistened a bright scarlet.

In fact, she actually seemed too completely glow. "Wow . . ." I muttered, looking at her in pure awe. "You're so beautiful."

She smiles and says, "Your quiet handsome tonight," and leaned towards me. We kissed, and I could still taste blood on her lips. I ran a hand threw her hair, pulled away and looked into her bright ice blue eyes,

A low footstep alerted us both. The moment we separated, two stakes whirled past where our hearts had been. Another slayer had to try and kill us, and to die trying.

He charged at me, and thrusted the stakes. Easily dodging them, I slam my fist into his chest, bones creaking and cracking, tendons popping. He gasped in pain as the breathe left his body. A few of his ribs had shattered, and a few splinters were bound to pierce organs. So then I put him out of his misery. I plunged my hand into his chest and tore out his heart.

Tossing the heart away, I felt light pulse in the back of my mind. "Ethan and Nathan are done as well," I tell Raven as we leave the alley.

"So now we go after the last two groups," she says, taking my hand. I nod, thinking about where they could be. Before she could say anything else, a light breeze blows past us. With it came the smell of garlic, gunpowder and wood. But it was coming from two directions.

"Damn it," I mutter, quickly leading Raven away and towards where Ethan and Nathan should be. She gives me a questioning glance. "They're here."

Her eyes widen in surprise as she asks, "So why are we running, then? Aren't we supposed to kill them?"

"Yeah, but we need to stick together now. The slayer groups are coming from two different directions. With guns," I replied, sensing the distance to the others closing.

Moments later, we reach them. They're both still feeding in the shadows. They don't notice us until they finish feeding seconds later.

"Oh. Dorian, Raven," Nathan said, trying to hide his surprise and failing miserably. "What brings you to us this early?"

"The last slayer groups are coming," Raven told him before I could reply. Taking a deep breath, she continues. "Coming here from two different directions."

"Great," Ethan muttered, clenching his fists. "Damned humans." Anger was radiating from him in huge torrents. He was almost visibly shaking with it, fists clenched together till his palms bled.

"Don't worry Ethan," I tell him, grinning slightly. "There's nothing to worry about. We'll kill them all."

"How?" he growled, seeming to grow even angrier.

"They're humans. All we have to do is get them to turn against each other," I reply calmly. "Then we can pick them off, one by one."

Slowly, very slowly as he thought it over, Ethan became calm once more. "How do you suppose we get them to turn on each other?" he asks.

"We mess with their senses," Raven stated. "Sight, smell, touch, taste, hearing. Make them think they see or hear us. Or make them think they smell rotting blood."

I smile at her and say, "Another great idea from you." A quick kiss and I turn my attention back to Ethan. "Is it good enough for you?"

Ethan nodded. "Sounds like a plan," he chuckled.

"Well then, let's end the hunt here as quickly as possible and move onto Africa," I say.

"Agreed," they all say.

One of the two groups is camped out a mile or so from the city. About twenty to twenty-five slayers. Decent odds too four vampires.

"So, apparently, they decided to make camp here," Nathan said, his anger rising slightly.

"Easier pickings and we don't have to worry about any average humans finding us," I chuckle, inhaling the scent of the slayers. Nathan also chuckled, his hunting instincts taking over.

"Shall we sneak around and attack from the sides?" Ethan asked, licking his lips in anticipation.

"No," I said. "We're going to fight them. We'll see just how skilled they are. It'll sweeten their blood." Nathan was smiling broadly, fangs fully extended and glistening. Ethan smiled lightly.

Raven looked at me and grinned. "Let's go," she said. Slowly, we all approached the camp, and split up.

A guard spotted me, and was about to shout a warning to the others until I was upon him. Grabbing his throat and squeezing, closing his windpipe, I slam my fist into his stomach. He gasped quietly and choked, unable to breathe. For a few moments he struggles, getting weaker until he goes limp.

I feed quickly and move to a tent. Two slayers attack at once. One stake brushes my shoulder, and the other my neck. Brutally, I slam their heads together. Not long after finishing them, I find a better slayer. Black trench coat, shirt, pants and boots. Deep-set dark hazel eyes and fair skin.

CHAPTER 10

His stake repeatedly missed my heart, but I always felt the tip brush my skin. Every time he'd miss, he'd jump back or to the side, avoiding the blows and preparing for his next strike if I came after him too soon. He was a very skilled slayer. I growl, baring my fangs.

He keeps his face blank as I leap towards him. The stake finally makes contact, but briefly and slightly. A small cut that heals within seconds. Pushing luck, he tried to thrust again. But before I could snap his arm, he drops to one knee, putting his momentum into it. I move.

The stake misses my heart, but plunges into my side. I hiss loudly in pain as he drove it in. He jumps back, along with his blood covered stake. Dropping to my knees, I clutch the wound, panting heavily.

"Dorian!!" Raven screams, appearing at my side. She notices my wound, the gaping hole on my side, and turns to the slayer. "You bastard!" she screeched and leaps towards him. He can tell immediately she's new and won't have to hold back. He can kill her with a single blow.

"No . . ." I gasp, slowly getting to my feet. The stake is quickly approaching her heart. I make a quick, hasty decision. Flitting in front of her, I grab his forearm as the stake plunges into my ribcage.

Both the slayer and Raven look at me in surprise. With my free arm, I grab the slayers head and squeeze, crushing his skull. Pulling him close and removing the stake, I bite into his neck. His blood floods my mouth and I eagerly gulp it down. Slowly, the wounds start to heal, but not as quickly as a small wound. It'd take a few minutes before there were gone completely.

"Dorian, why'd you do that? You could've been killed!" she cries, eyes watering.

"If I hadn't . . . you would've . . . been killed," I tell her. "The stake was perfectly lined with your heart. He almost . . . took what's most precious to me." I look into her eyes, seeing her fear and worry.

Her ice blue eyes, so mesmerizing, held the red dots of an Original. Looking into her eyes, deep, consuming . . .

Her lips press up against mine. It sends a powerful electrical charge threw me. I kiss her back, and it grows stronger. Our kiss is like being in the core of an electric storm. It flows around, over and threw us.

It takes all my will to end it, though I longed for it to continue. It had the same effect on her. "Later, my love," I whispered to her. She nods her head, and together, we both started killing the remaining slayers.

When we met up with Ethan and Nathan, ten or so minutes later, they looked at my torn shirt and almost completely healed wound. "What the hell happened to you two?" Ethan asked me.

"A slayer. A very skilled and smart slayer," I replied. I tell them about the encounter, and lead them to the body. "Turn away for me," I tell them, examining the dead man's clothes.

When they do, I strip out of my clothes and put his on. "Much better," I say, and they turn to face me.

"Indeed," Raven says playfully and steps into my arms.

"A suiting outfit for you, Dorian," Nathan tells me, humor in his eyes. I chuckle lightly and just simply enjoy the feeling of Raven in my arms.

But a few moments, we had to end the embrace and continued on to the next slayer group. They were only a few miles away, the guards looking sleepy and exhausted.

CHAPTER 11

"We'll be splitting into two groups," I tell them. "Be cautious, as well. Raven and I will start from the side. You and Ethan come from the other."

"What if we encounter a slayer like the one you fought?" Ethan asks, and Raven tenses. "How'll we be able to protect ourselves?"

I chuckle lightly and answer, "That's why we're splitting into two groups. One of you can try and distract him while the other sneaks around him to do some damage, or just kill him. It's just that simple."

Ethan just nods, Nathan grins wildly. *It seems he has insatiable appetite for battle*, I thought with a light chuckle.

With one quick nod, we split apart and move to the sides of the camp. Two guards keeping watch this time. But it didn't matter. We leapt upon them in a third of a second and within seconds they were dead.

Not long after that, we were going from tent to tent, draining each and every slayer. None were AB, but it was still a delicious banquet.

Ethan and Nathan found us as we were finishing feeding. Nathan sighs and said, "Damn. I was hoping to find a slayer who could actually put up a decent fight. But no. All that was here are these pathetic, weak fools who shouldn't even be hunting anything. Hell, even a deer would put up more of a fight than all of these weaklings put together."

"You still might, Nathan," I tell him. "We can finally take our hunt to Africa. Maybe you'll find your ultimate foe there, or in Europe."

His eyes light up with eager desire. Ethan rolls his eyes, but smiles. Raven smiles as well. "So, how are we going to get there?" she asked.

Glancing at Ethan, I ask, "How far are we from your jet?"

For a moment or so, he's silent, thinking. "Two, maybe three days," he replied. I sighed. *Two or three days to get to the jet*, I thought, *and a couple more just to get there.*

"Um . . . the sun's starting to rise," Raven warns. Swearing, we all look up to see the horizon lighting up. Growling, I look around.

A tree catches my eye. A hole burrows deep beneath it, down to the roots. The scent coming from it says it's a snake den, but snakes don't mind vampires. "We'll have to rest here," I tell them, quickly widening the hole. After about five or seven feet, I dig right about nine feet, and finally widen it for all of us to fit into.

The others quickly enter the burrow, and once we're all comfortable, use Power to move the dirt to cover us, and drift into sleep . . .

The instant the sun disappears, we rise from our earthen graves. The sky is still a light purple, but the sun can't harm us.

"Let's get going," I say, taking Raven's hand, and running, the others behind us. Within moments, we hit flitting speed.

It only took us two days to reach the jet. Marius and Alexander were the first to notice our approach. They seemed slightly surprised to see us. "What are you all doing back so soon?" Alexander asked.

"We need to take another flight. A longer one," Ethan replied.

"Where do you want to go this time?" Marius asked, gesturing for the others to check the plane.

"We need to go to Africa," I answered. "As quickly as possible."

They looked at us with raised eyebrows but don't ask any more questions. "Give a few minutes," they say and enter the control room. Moments later, they return.

"The jet will be ready to leave in about twenty minutes," Alexander tells us, before entering the plane to do a systems check.

Nathan sighed. "We should find a way to tell them we're coming earlier," he grumbles to himself. Ethan shakes his head and chuckles at him.

Raven takes my hand and instantly that same electrical feeling engulfed us. It's stronger than before, and much thicker.

By the time we get onto the jet, it becomes unbearable and irresistible. We instantly take one of the rooms, and mate. It was perfect. We were so in synch it was crazy. It was the best time I had in all my countless millennia of walking this world.

A few days later, the jet lands at a South African town, just too avoid immediately running into slayers.

Both Nathan and Ethan sigh and stretch once we're out. They only time either of them had woken during the entire flight was to drink blood wine.

"It feels good to move again," Ethan groaned, cracking his arms and back.

Raven and I simply watch them, having spent most of the flight awake. She leans against me, her arm around my waist and mine around hers.

CHAPTER 12

When they finally finished a few moments later, the jet had taken off again and was heading back to the states.

"Are you two ready to go yet?" Raven asks impatiently. "We've been for twenty minutes already."

"Yeah, we're ready," Nathan replies, lifting up his bag of supplies. "Let's go hunting for some slayers." As always, there's a grin on his face at the thought of a decent death match.

As a gentle breeze blows past us, it carries the smells of human blood, smoke, ash, et cetera. It's a change for us. The airs absent of the smells of silver, garlic and gunpowder but I'm not surprised.

African slayers probably used ash wood stakes alone, maybe occasionally using silver and garlic, which would be nearly impossible to smell with the scent of ash constantly in the air.

But as we get closer to the town, a black hurricane of rage and pure hate surges threw me swiftly and violently, as my blood seems to freeze within my veins, stiff and thick, heavy. Raven feels it too and reacts the same way: freezes.

"What's wrong?" Ethan asks but we didn't need to answer him as he and Nathan smell it. Old, very ancient blood. Older and more ancient than their own. It's the scent only an Original has.

"They will *not* do this," I snarl, moving more quickly and with real purpose and urgency. Raven seems almost as angry as I am. "Kill everyone you see. Man, woman and child. Slayer and normal human alike."

It'd seem the entire town has gathered in the center to watch the execution. A woman was strapped down on a wooden platform above a blazing, white hot fire, an African slayer speaking to the spectators. I don't hesitate, to angry and way to pissed to waste time. Flitting threw the crowd; I grab the slayers neck and twist in one swift movement. Instantly, Ethan and Nathan beginning killing all those who've gathered to watch, while Raven untied the woman's bindings. The woman has dark blonde hair reaching her shoulders, and she has beautiful cobalt blue eyes. In them are the red dots that mark an Original.

"Thank you," she says to me and Rave in a sweet, calming voice like liquid gold, noticing us as others of the same creation.

"No problem," Raven says as I join the onslaught. Only a few remain, but they're all slayers. Pretty decent slayers, as well.

But not skilled enough. About five or seven minutes later, they lay on the ground, dead.

Once we're sure no one has survived, I turn to the woman and tell her, "My name is Dorian, and this's my mate, Raven. Our two companions are the Ancients, Ethan and Nathan."

She nods at each of us and says, "I'm Chandler. I'd come to Africa with a hunting party, but all the others were killed." She doesn't seem very surprised, or upset by that, which meant . . .

"Your hunting party was made of newborns? Inexperienced vampires?" I ask her, raising an eyebrow.

"Yeah," she sighs, closing her eyes. "It was a night or so ago now. We were looking for a place to rest and hide from the sun when they came. Maybe twenty or more, I can't remember. All the others were either staked or left to burn in the rising light of the sun."

It's a brutal image as we all imagine it. "They call *us* monsters," Ethan mutters.

"So, anyway, what brings you all her?" she asks.

"To rid the world of slayers. To free us all from the ever constant threat of being hunted by a disgraceful human," I reply. "We've killed all of them in the States. Now it's Africa, and then onto Europe."

She nods her head, seeming to think something over in her head. A moment or so later, she asks, "Do you mind if I tag along? There aren't many slayers left here."

"Sure," Raven says. Ethan and Nathan glance at her, than at me with questioning looks. I just shrug. It didn't matter to me.

"So, how many groups do you think are left here?" I ask.

"Maybe two or three. With the group you all just killed . . . most likely one or two now," Chandler replies.

We all sigh and smile. *Not too many slayers left to kill*, I thought.

A quick glance up at the sky reveals that the sun will be rising soon. We all hurry into a nearby building, boarding up the windows to keep out the light. Once it's completely dark, we close our eyes and soon fall asleep.

Nightfall, the moment the sun disappears in the distance, we rise and move on. Hours pass before we reach the next town.

We don't encounter any slayers here as we feed. Once full, we move on once again. But we encounter a group about a mile from the town. Twenty of them, carrying two stakes each.

Sighing, I tell the others, "Let's get this over with quickly." There was no hesitation as we slaughter them. About a minute passes, and they're dead. Short and sweet, nothing more.

Nathan sighs, half pleasantly and half annoyed. "Where the bloody hell are all the good slayers at, eh?" he mutters to himself as we walk.

"Why are you so eager to fight? Aren't you worried that they'll burn you over an open fire and stake you? Or starve you for days and drag you out into the daylight?" Chandler asks him.

"Nope," he tells her simply. "Dorian is the only one among us whose fight a truly experienced slayer, so far. Managed to stake him, an Original, twice. That's the kind of slayer whom I desire to fight. Someone who can offer me a real fight." His eyes gleam brightly as he smirks.

Raven shudders, remembering that night. Chandler glanced at me, and before she can speak I tell her, "Yes, it's true. But the stake only pierced my right ribs and side."

CHAPTER 13

"How'd a human manage to stake you twice?" she inquires.

Sighing slightly, I reply, "The first time was probably luck alone. If I hadn't gotten between the slayer and Raven, she would've been killed." I wrap an arm around her and she leans into me. "So, instead of piercing her heart, the stake plunged here, into my right rib cage." I place my hand exactly where the stake had hit, middle of them.

She winces slightly. Raven adds, "Before the slayer could react, Dorian crushed his skull."

That makes everyone smile. After a few seconds of silence, Nathan asks, "So, where shall we go from here?"

Dylan Wetzel

All of are silent, deep in thought. A few moments later, Chandler suggests, "We can go north. I'm pretty sure there's a group up there."

"Are you sure?" Ethan asks.

"Pretty sure," she answers.

Raven says, "Well then, let's get going. The longer we stay here, the more likely they are to move."

She was right. So, after another moments silence, I tell them, "If we do find them, remember to never drop your guard," and then we all make our way north. Within seconds, we're flitting.

We only stopped at villages every two or three hours as we headed north. No one seemed to notice.

Two days pass until we come to the next town, at early dawn.

"About time," Nathan mutters. "I was really getting tired of just constant sand and running." Ethan snickers silently.

"Yeah, well now we need to find a resting place," I say. "Sun will be rising soon."

Chandler gestures with a hand to an abounded building. "Why not there?" she suggests. "I highly doubt we'll encounter humans, much less slayers, in there. In the dark."

As I think it over, I allow my senses to range outward. The sound of a heart and the smell of blood are quite close. But, looking around, I don't see anything. Sighing, I reply, "Alright." We quickly make our way inside, just as the sun finally rises.

CHAPTER 14

I heard them gathering outside the building, around maybe midday or early evening. But the sun would be at its highest point, and they knew it. Sounded like at least ten or so slayers.

"What?" Ethan growls quietly, but instantly freezes when the sound and smell hit him. Quickly we wake the others and move deeper into the shadows, hiding ourselves for when they came in.

Moments later, they spill in, stakes ready. My guess was off by a little. There are only eight slayers. I glance at the others. They nod at me, and silently, we all hide in a spot that offers the best advantage for us to attack from.

As they slowly spread out, after lighting torches, they begin searching. Two of them stay by the door.

The moment one gets close enough to me, I quickly leap up, snap a man's neck, and pull him into the shadows. I toss the torch in the opposite direction, to avoid being found while I feed.

The others had grabbed a slayer as well, draining their life away. It didn't go unnoticed. Only one human was left to continue, and he's visibly shaking. The other two aren't as nervous, but the smell of fear fills the room. They're all on edge.

Barley a whisper, I say, "Let's keep the searcher for questioning. Kill the other two." They nod in agreement and we move in a single, blurry movement.

Chandler, Ethan and Nathan go for the two by the door while Raven and I subdue the slayer.

Instantly, panic coursed threw him and he began to speak quickly. I didn't understand a word he was saying. It's all in African. But before I can speak if he speaks English, he freezes at the sound of his dead, drained companions.

Fear fills his eyes as the others join us. When he looks at me, I ask, "Do you speak English, human?" He shakes his head. Sighing, I squeeze my eyes shut.

"I speak African," Chandler tells me.

I instantly open my eyes, giving her my full, undivided attention. "Ask him how many slayers, where they're at, and then put him out of his misery," I tell her.

As she begins questioning him, I look out the heavily boarded windows, making sure there aren't any others waiting outside. I see no one, but to absolutely sure, I open my senses to their fullest extent.

The only sounds come from Chandler as she speaks, the slayers heartbeat and the rush of his blood threw his veins, and his answers; crackling fires, and other, more distant hearts.

All I can smell is fresh, living blood; ancient blood; smoke, cooking meat and ash.

The sound of his scream and his neck breaking is like explosion in my head. Cringing, I cover my ears; quickly reigning my senses back in to more endurable heights.

"He said this was the last African group," she tells me with a smirk. We all sigh, grateful that we're almost finished this long journey.

"Now, our next destination is Europe," Raven says, taking my hand. I nod, and kiss her forehead gently.

"Then, after that, it's to our last and final destination, China," Ethan mutters, stifling a yawn.

Nathan says, "Most likely than not, they'll all be weak and pathetic. None of them will have enough skills, brains or anything to pose a threat to us. Hell, even a deer puts up more of a fight than they do." Like usual, his desire to fight was making him angry.

"You don't know that," I tell him. "They might be the best we encounter." He doesn't seem convinced, but within moments, we drift asleep.

CHAPTER 15

About two or three days later, we enter Europe. We're in a very large forest, the moon waning in the sky.

"How far do you think we are from a city or town?" Raven asks as we walk, silently as ghosts.

A light, gently breeze was passing by us, and we all inhaled. It carries the scent of animals, freshly spilled blood and torn flesh, tree bark, sap . . . and blood. Human blood. My mouth instantly goes dry, and my throat blazes like a white hot wildfire.

"AB negative . . ." Chandler purred, almost moaned. The instinct to hunt was growing stronger and stronger, taking over. Unable to resist, we all take off, flitting towards the exact place of the smell.

A human had made a camp a few miles away. We reach it within about two minutes, and don't waste time opening the tent. Nathan goes in first, followed by Ethan.

Nathan was just about to bite the human when he's suddenly kicked in the gut. The force and surprise push both him and Ethan out.

Emerging from the tent is a slayer, and thrusts two stakes, one at each of them. Nathan and Ethan dodged them with ease.

A vicious smile worked its way onto Nathan's face. To us, he snarls, "Do not interfere! He is mine!!" and then lunges at the slayer. The slayer dodges easily, but Nathan manages to pull his cloak off.

He's tall, about six feet five inches, Very muscular. Skin the color of ivory. Cropped, light brown hair. Deep set dark blue eyes, and low cheek bones.

Ethan, Chandler, Raven and I watch as they circle each other, eyes locked. The slayer holds the stakes near his chest, poised to strike; Nathan's hands were curled into claws.

It's so deathly silent; it seemed that even the night dared to breathe.

Then the death match began.

Lashing out with his right stake, the slayer takes a quick step forward. Nathan catches him by the wrist and swung his left hand up. The other stake slashed down it.

Growling, he pulls the slayers fingers out of place violently. The slayer doesn't even wince, nor does he drop the stake. He quickly steps away from Nathan and shoves his fingers back into place.

Chuckling, Nathan says, "I'll give you this much. Your good, and can handle pain. Most admirable. But one way or another, you're going to die." His tone and facial expression quickly harden, more serious. "Your days of killing of us are over." He lunged at him again.

This time, however, the slayer steps forward and drops to one knee, and thrusted. A stake plunges into Nathan's left rib cage, just barely missing his heart, while the other plunged into his lower right side.

Nathan growls, baring his fangs. Then the slayer speaks. In a deep, rich voice he says, "It seems that you'll be the one dying tonight, monster. I'll never stop hunting you creatures down." Quickly he pulls his stakes free and aims one directly at Nathan's heart, and goes for the kill.

But the moment he removed them, Nathan had flitted behind him. When the slayer realized it, it was too late. Nathan viciously bites into his neck, puncturing an artery. The slayer gasps in pain, and tries to break away. He wasn't able too. Nathan had wrapped his arms tightly around his prey. The richest, sweetest prey he'd had in a long time. Like me, when I'd been staked, blood helped speed up his healing.

His wounds were pretty much completely healed now. All that was left were two pink circular marks on him. A smile on his face, he says, "About damn time I find a good slayer." We all chuckle, me and Ethan rolling our eyes.

"At least we now know that Europe may offer better slayers," I said.

"Good for Nathan," Ethan says. He chuckles. We all knew that Nathan would be, more or less, less angry as long as the other slayers offer him as much of a fight as this one did.

I was a little worried, though. *If we do encounter a group this skilled, how much danger would Raven be in?* I though with a shudder.

"What's wrong?" she asks me once we're walking again. There's a deep concern in her eyes.

"Nothing. It's nothing," I whisper, wrapping an arm around her waist and hers around mine. *No matter what,* I thought, *I will protect her at any coast.*

A few more hours passed until the sun rose. Like before, we dug holes in the ground to rest in.

CHAPTER 16

Over the next few nights, we encountered multiple slayer groups. Sometimes three or four per night, a few nights in a row. We killed at least five groups of them. "Three or four more left," Raven says after we finished feeding one night as we were resting.

All of us, especially Nathan, were in a good mood. We were very close to achieving our goal. Only a week, maybe even two weeks, and our kind would be safe from slayers.

"Jordan said some would, or might, be in China," she continues. "Should we continue looking here or move onto China?"

"To China," Ethan replies.

Nathan and Chandler say together, "Either way works."

They all turn towards me. It doesn't take me very long to make a decision. "China it is, then," I say, getting up. Instantly Raven's at my side.

"To China," she agrees with a smile.

The others smirk and soon, we're flitting threw the wilderness again.

We ran for countless hours, the scenery rarely changing. The moon was visible before we started to flit. But now it's gone, and the horizon is slowly brightening up with the rising sun.

"Time to rest," I tell them, quickly slowly down. They stop almost exactly the same time I do. I look around, trying to find a descent resting place.

Nothing to use as a resting place, or anything immediately to shield us from the sunlight. Closing my eyes, I channel Power threw my body, down to my feet and into the ground before me.

The ground before me caves inward, about two feet deep, and four feet wide, coffin shaped.

"How'd you do that?" Chandler asks curiously.

"Power," I replied, taking Raven's hand. "Channel it threw your body, down to your feet and into the ground." As we lay down, we hear the ground caving in around us and felt Power pulsing in the ground.

Once they lay in theirs, she asks, "Now what?"

"Then you simply use that Power in the ground to raise more dirt," I answer her, just as Raven and mines refills.

A moment or so later, we hear and feel it three other times.

Within moments, all of us drift into sleep.

CHAPTER 17

We rise the moment the sun completely vanishes in the distances. The night is surprisingly quiet. I pause, listening. The others, when they emerge, notice. Before they can ask me anything, I hold up a finger for silence.

Immediately, they too noticed it was by far too silent. No birds chirping or attending their nests, no animals scurrying about. Even the wind was still. Very slowly, I allow my senses to range outward, trying to detect any sign of life or anything.

I catch something . . . unusual. A heartbeat. A very slow one at that, and it wasn't any of ours. Too slow to be human.

It's a vampire heartbeat. But the smells that go with it make no sense. Silver and ash wood. *Why would another vampire smell like that?* I thought.

A third of a second later, I heard the new vampire quickly approaching. My defensive instincts quickly take over as I go to meet our unexpected guest. Naturally, the others follow me.

When I see it is, I froze. Both from disbelief and surprise.

The very first slayer group leader I'd encountered, and thought I'd killed. Yet here he was, now the thing he hated.

I snarl at him viciously, and he simply smiles, fangs just barely visible behind his lips. "It's about time I found you," he said, still wearing that irritating smile. His light gray hair was messier that it was the last time I saw it, and his eyes darker.

"How'd you become a vampire? Better yet, how the *hell* are you still alive?" I demand. "I was sure you were dead."

"That's none of your concern," he cackles. "Besides, you're about to die. No point telling you anything." He drew a stake from a holster on his right hip, a silver tip and handle, and crouches down, ready to leap.

Mirroring his crouch, I tell the others "Don't interfere in this. He is mine. All I need you all to do is protect Raven." They nod in agreement.

Then we begin.

Leaping forward, he lashes out with the stake. I easily dodge it, but then he thrusts it quicker, aimed at my heart.

I crouch down again and lean away. The stake just barely misses my shoulder. He growls lightly and swings a leg at my head. Grabbing his ankle, I twist until I hear a satisfying snap.

Snarling like a wild animal, he leaps back a few feet. Quickly he snaps his ankle back into place. *This seemed very odd. That would've been easy, though painful, to heal,* I thought.

So, why'd he do it like that? It's a mystery to me. A very annoying one. Any vampire, new or old, could heal just about any wound. Injured bones could be healed, over time, with the smallest bit of Power . . .

"Ahh," I whispered, finally understanding. If he had no power, that meant he hadn't been feeding.

"What?" he growls. Now that I knew this, I could see the signs of starvation upon him. Deep dark eyes, sunken in with hunger, and a waxy tint in his pale skin.

"How thirsty are you?" I asked him. He stiffens. Chuckling, I add, "Is your throat blazing constantly? Are you always hungry?"

He takes a while to reply, "Yes. The thirst burns white hot every day. I have never fed, and never will. Just because I'm a vampire . . . doesn't mean I should kill for a meal." Again, he leaps at me.

His arm goes back and then he thrusted. I simply push his arm away and grab him by the throat. He snarled, trying to break free. He couldn't, I made sure of that.

"You're a fool," I tell him. "Blood is what'll keep you alive. It'll give you strength, power. You don't have to kill. Drink what you need and leave if you want." His eyes widened in surprise. "Humans aren't our only prey, though they taste best and they're blood gives the most power. We can live on animal blood, as well."

He was silent, seeming to think. But I interrupt him. Lifting him up off the ground, he instantly started trying to pry my hand away. I slammed him onto the ground violently. He grunts slightly and shoves me away.

He's on his feet in a fraction of a second, fangs bared and stake risen, ready to strike. "Why, then, don't you feed from animals? Why only humans?" he demands of me.

Shrugging slightly, never taking my eyes off him, I reply, "I just told you. Human blood tastes better and it offers more strength and power."

He snapped, "But it's not enough for you. You enjoy feeding from and killing humans! I won't become a monster!!" He takes a few deep breaths before adding, "The one bit of respect I'll show you . . . is my name. It's Andrew."

He charged me this time, holding the stake low. When he's about a foot and a half from me, the stake comes up.

I dodged, but he didn't stop. But I quickly realized his real target.

It was Raven.

Rage and panic surged threw me as I roar, "No!!" and leap after him. The others quickly circle Raven, baring their fangs and snarling at Andrew.

Suddenly, when I was about half a foot from him, and he's seven feet from the others, he whirls around, and then the stake is soaring towards me.

I felt the tip pierce the middle of my chest but plunged inward to the left. I gasped painfully as the tip brushes my heart. He tries to plunge it in even deeper, to pierce my heart, but luckily he couldn't.

CHAPTER 18

When he finally accepted that the stake couldn't go any deeper, he pulled it free, dripping blood. Then, as I drop to my knees, panting and gasping in pain, he kicks me onto my side. Once again, he takes aim . . .

Then I black out.

All I felt was pain. It was unbearable. I couldn't see, hear or smell. The only sense I had was touch, but all I could feel was pain.

Days could've passed. Weeks, months, or even years before I finally opened my eyes again.

Raven held me in her arms, eyes full of panic and wearing, tears running down her cheeks. The others weren't far away, looking just as worried.

The moment they all notice I'm waking, all of them sighed in relief.

"Dorian!" Raven cried, staring into my eyes. "I'm so glad you're alive! I thought he'd killed you!!" She was absolutely upset. It broke my heart to see her like this, so hurt and vulnerable.

I gently stroke her cheek and whisper, "Don't fret . . . my love. I'll always . . . be at your . . . side." She leans down and kisses me lovingly.

The electric feeling that shot threw us in that one kiss was enough to get me onto my feet. Raven raised her eyebrows. I smile lightly at her, and then realize the pain was gone.

The moment I look down, Chandler tell me, "It's healed. Raven and I gave you some of our blood. Ethan and Nathan fed you at least three bottles of blood wine."

Nodding, I then ask, "What happened to . . . him?"

There was a silent moment before my question was answered. "We . . . dealt with him the instant you fell," Nathan answers. "Ethan and I tore them apart. To make sure, we buried each limb a mile apart, and three feet deep."

I sighed, squeezing my eyes shut. "Don't worry, Dorian. We don't think any less of you. No one could've seen what he was planning," Ethan says.

"He's right," Raven agrees. "We're all glad that we managed to save you."

Nathan searched his bag for a moment before saying, "Here. Drink this," and tossed me a bottle.

Catching it in midair, I ask, "What type is it?"

"Clean, AB negative," he replies. I give him a quick grin, and uncork the bottle, and raised it to my lips to drink. The taste is so rich, so very sweet . . .

CHAPTER 19

A few nights later, we reached the Great Wall of China, which we all easily jumped over, and kept on going.

The smell of bamboo, water and animals is thick as we walk through a jungle. There was a light rainfall, but we didn't mind.

An hour or so later, we come across a small market.

"Anyone thirty?" I asked with a chuckle. They grin, nodding in agreement. "Well then, let's hunt."

Quickly and silently as ghosts, we move through the market, not killing anyone for a change. But yards outside the market, we stumble upon a slayer group. Ten slayers, each with two stakes and garlic. It also seemed there garlic smeared on the stakes as well, making them all that much more lethal.

Nathan shuddered and said, "What a disgusting, repulsive aroma." Ethan and the others nod their heads in agreement.

Without warning, they all circle us, spread out as to not get in each other's way. "This should be interesting," I said sarcastically. Ethan doesn't seem very happy, perhaps afraid he'll end up in a situation like my previous one; Nathan looked excited; Chandler and Raven seemed nervous.

Then they made their move. Two slayers charged at me. I flitted between them, tore free two stakes and plunged them both into their skulls. Unable to resist the smell of fresh blood, I begin to feed.

Distantly, I'm aware of the others as they handled their slayers. Then I realized Raven was fighting, as well.

Instantly, I looked around for her. She had already killed the two that had been her opponents, and was feeding on the second. Nathan and Chandler had simply killed theirs. Ethan had torn their throats open and broke their necks.

"That wasn't even worth any effort," Nathan sighs. "A human could've killed these pathetic, miserable wretches with one arm tied behind their back."

"That was too easy," Chandler agreed. "These slayers are absolutely pathetic."

"They didn't meet your expectations?" I ask them sarcastically. Nathan growls lightly, and Chandler rolls her eyes. I just chuckle.

Ethan sighed and said, "After all those experienced slayers, I thought all the others to follow would be just as good, or more skilled."

Raven says, "At least no one got hurt."

Her words brought a strange silence, remembering the times when Nathan and I had been staked. Not very pleasant memories to have.

A moment or so later, Chandler asks, "So, are we going to stay here, sulking? Or are we going to hurry up and finish our journey?"

Glancing at Raven, she grins at me and together, we reply, "Let's get going, then."

The others look at us, seeming to have come back to the present from where their thoughts had taken them.

I raise an eyebrow, and they grin. Within moments, we're on the move again. Our direction, northwest.

CHAPTER 20

Over the next three nights, two more slayer groups were found. They put up a decent fight for about three minutes. But in the end, we killed them, like all the others.

However, one of them, a slayer we decided to question, told us that there is only one last group, in Southern China. He also revealed that they are the most experienced and skilled of them all.

Dusk. We were in another forest. It isn't as humid as it could be, but we could tell that the temperature was quickly dropping. Not that we noticed it.

Nathan says, "I absolutely can't wait to find them." His smile revealed his fangs, his eyes full of desire, eagerness and lust for battle.

"Me either," I agree. "I just want to finish this as soon as possible. Then I know we'll be safe." Subconsciously, I take Raven's hand, fingers entwined.

"I just want to be with you," she whispered to me, giving my hand a gently squeeze, and grinned at me.

Grinning in return, I squeeze her hand back and say, "Likewise, my love," and give her a quick kiss.

"So I'm guessing that she'll be with you when we return?" Ethan asks, smiling slightly.

"Of course," we say together, and they chuckle.

"Where will you be going?" Nathan asks Chandler.

She shrugs and replies, "I don't really have a specific place in mind." Then, with a playful smile and tone, asks him, "Why?"

He grins and answers, "I'm in need of female companionship. It's been a very long since I was last with a woman. You seem to enjoy a good battle as much as I do. I'd like to have you forever at my side."

She blushes a little. Ethan, Raven and I chuckle. Nathan smiles broadly and raised an eyebrow. Her blush deepens ever so slightly, and pretended to think it over. Then she says, "Oh, what the hell. I will." Nathan smiles fully, and then kisses her. She kisses him back, wrapping an arm around him.

Ethan coughs, and then starts snickering. Chandler ended the kiss, but held his hand and stood quite close to him.

"Let's see if you two lovebirds can keep up!" I said, taking Raven's hand.

"We'll fly right past you two," Nathan growls sarcastically.

One silent moment, and then we're running, Ethan right behind us.

In the end, about a minute later, Chandler and Raven bring our little race to an end. Nathan sighed. "Did that little run make you tired?" Raven asked him.

He rolls his eyes and answers, "Of course not. I'm just wondering when we'll encounter the last group of slayers."

"Me too," Chandler agrees. "The sooner we finish this hunt, the sooner we can finally return to where ever you all came from."

"The United States," I tell her.

Before she can say anything, we heard them. Soft, quick footsteps in the distance, but not heading towards us. They're moving east. Their scent is human, tainted strongly by all the vampires they'd killed. Ash wood stakes with silver tips and nothing more.

"Damnit," I muttered, instantly moving after them. Within seconds, we're silently leaping from branch to branch, only feet behind them.

Just four slayers this time. Two ashy-blondes, one black haired and one with silver hair. They're all very tanned, very muscular, and pretty tall. About five feet nine inches.

"Where do you think they're going?" Raven whispers.

"I don't know," I whisper back. "Let's follow them and find out. Maybe they're looking for vampires to kill. If they are, we'll give them one hell of a fight."

CHAPTER 21

We followed them for a while, all the way back to a camp. Obviously, it was theirs. They quickly had a blazing fire, and soon, the smell of roasting meat filled the air.

"Gross," Nathan hissed, plugging his nose closed.

I nodded my head in agreement. "Now, we kill them," I tell the others. "Show no hesitation, and do not prolong a fight. End it as soon as you can."

"Agreed," Ethan said.

Nathan, with an exaggerated sigh, says, "I'll try not to prolong it any longer than necessary."

Chandler laughs quietly as she says, "I'll try not too, as well."

"But there's only four," Raven pointed out. "Do you expect me to stay here?"

"No," I replied, turning to face her. "But you won't be fighting. I will not risk you getting killed. Please. Just let us do the fighting."

"One condition," she says.

"Anything," I said.

"Just . . . please, try to not get hurt," she whimpered, fear in her deep, icy blue eyes.

I stroked her cheek and tell her, "For you, I promise, I'll try to avoid any injury they'll try to inflict upon me."

She nods slowly. To the others, I say, "Let's get this over with. There's only two hours left until sunrise, so we'd better finish it quickly."

Nodding, we leave the tree, and approach the camp from different directions. Two feet from it, the silver haired one emerges, stakes held high. Light, hazel eyes stare into my own eyes.

Then, surprisingly, he spoke. "My name is Dimitri. What would yours be, vampire?" he asks me in a clear, rich and velvety voce.

"Dorian," I replied, giving him a small bow. Even more astonishing, he bows to me in return.

Then he instantly leaps at me, stakes lashing out. Dodging them, I go for his throat. He quickly sidesteps and thrusts a stake forward.

I crouch and grab his wrist, then kick his legs to the side. He grunts slightly as he smacks onto the ground. He's up in seconds.

The stake plunges towards my heart again. I slap his arm away. He takes a step forward and the other stake soars towards me. Kicking him feet away, I flit towards him. His leg lashes out, with a large, silver switchblade attached to it with chains.

It just barely cut both of my thighs. This healed almost immediately. Grabbing his ankle, I lift him up off the ground and toss him feet away. Before he even hits the ground, I slam his head down onto it hard.

He gasps in pain but still manages to slash my hand open, deeply. I growl slightly. Within seconds, my hand's healed. A leg pushes my right leg back and I fall.

Snarling, I grab both of his wrists, and pull him down with me. Then, as he's falling, I bite into his neck. O negative. I eagerly gulp down every drop in seconds. The moment I pull away and get to my feet, Raven has her arms around me in a tight embrace.

CHAPTER 22

A n hour before sunrise. The four slayers are dead, burning in the fire. None of us had been injured severely. Just a few cuts and scratches that had already healed themselves.

We all sigh happily inside the large tent. "Tomorrow, we finally head home," Ethan says, sighing happily again.

"I'm sure we're all grateful for that," Nathan said. Chandler was sitting beside him, her head on his chest.

"Indeed," I agreed, holding Raven in my arms. *Now she'll always be safe*, I thought. Within these peaceful moments, I close my eyes and drift into the most peaceful sleep I'd had in a long time.

At nightfall, we were all ready to leave, and we weren't going to stay here any longer. We spend the nights running, stopping only to feed when we needed, to rest, and to sleep during the day.

Within a few nights, we reached the Pacific sea. We swim out to deeper warms, take as deep breathes as we can, and submerge ourselves, hidden beneath the water's surface.

About a week or so later, we rose at the beach of Ocean City, Maryland.

"Anyone want to buy some stuff while we're here?" Ethan asked, cackling.

"Not really," Raven said. "But I would like to feed." Her stomach gives a light growl to prove it.

"As do I," Chandler, Nathan and I agree.

Quickly, we all went off to hunt. Ethan, Chandler and Nathan went to search the boardwalk for a meal while Raven and I crept from room to room in the nearby hotels, searching for sleeping guests to feed from.

About an hour passes, and with our hunger sedated, we're on our way again. Another day passes and we had finally reached Ethan's and Nathan's private club. Immediately, Ethan goes to relieve Alex of his duties, while Nathan and Chandler go to his room.

Raven and I linger for a bit before claiming a room of our own.

We collapsed onto the soft, comfy bed in each other's arms, kissing. "Now I can finally keep you to myself," she said between kisses.

"Forever and ever," I agreed.